TRIPLET TROUBLE
and
the Pizza Party

There are more books about
the Tucker Triplets!

TRIPLET TROUBLE
and
the Pizza Party

by Debbie Dadey and Marcia Thornton Jones
Illustrated by John Speirs

A
LITTLE APPLE
PAPERBACK

SCHOLASTIC INC.
New York Toronto London Auckland Sydney

ISBN 0-590-90729-8

12 11 10 9 8 7 6 5 4 3 2 1   6 7 8 9/9 0 1/0

Printed in the U.S.A.   40

First Scholastic printing, December 1996

To Randy and Melissa Thornton — a wonderful brother and sister-in-law — MTJ

In memory of a good dog and friend, Cleo — DD

Contents

Trouble

"Watch out!" I yelled. A paper airplane flew past Ashley Tucker's head. It barely missed her long blond hair.

Ashley stood up and looked at her sister. Alex Tucker was the one who threw the plane.

"You hit me on purpose!" Ashley cried and poked Alex on the shoulder.

"I didn't hit you," Alex said, poking back. "I missed you by a mile."

A couple of kids in our second-grade class yelled out, "Fight! Fight!"

"Stop!" Adam Tucker said. "Mr. Parker is back." Adam Tucker is Ashley and Alex's brother. The Tuckers are triplets. Adam is very smart and almost always right. This time he was definitely right.

Mr. Parker had been standing outside the door talking to Barbara's mother. Now he was standing inside the door. He was looking at us and he was not happy.

"Oh, no!" I whispered. "We're in big trouble." My name is Sam Johnson, and with the Tucker Triplets in my class, we get in trouble a lot.

Mr. Parker rubbed his chin and cleared his throat. I thought that he was going to yell at us. But Mr. Parker didn't say a word. He wrote on the board. I couldn't believe what he wrote: PIZZA PARTY

"Hurrah!" the kids in my class yelled. Alex yelled the loudest of all.

Mr. Parker held up his hand. "Not so fast. This is a pizza party you must earn."

4

Everybody in the class groaned, especially Alex.

Mr. Parker kept talking and held up a big jar. "The closer it gets to Christmas, the more trouble you seem to be getting into. Every time the whole class is being good, I'll put a red Christmas ball into this jar. When it's full, we'll have a pizza party."

Everybody cheered again. But I didn't. The jar looked awfully big. Was there any way the Tucker Triplets could stay out of trouble for that long?

2

Good Reminders

The next day I stopped by the Tuckers' house on my way to school. I always walk to school with the triplets. They live four houses away.

Alex was standing on the front porch waiting for me.

Alex doesn't always like being a triplet. She likes to look different. That morning she had tied little silver jingle bells to her sweater's buttons. She even tied them to her shoelaces! Alex turned around fast so I could see her hair better. When she turned around she jingled. She had twenty tiny jingle bells tied to twenty tiny ponytails.

"I don't think Mr. Parker will like your jingle bells," I told her.

Alex smiled so big I saw the space where her tooth used to be. "Yes, he will," she told me. "Lots of people wear jingle bells during Christmas. I even saw jingle-bell necklaces at the drugstore."

"But Mr. Parker wants us to be quiet," I reminded her. "Jingle bells aren't quiet."

"Mr. Parker likes lots of Christmas decorations. He hung garlands over the blackboard. He hung candy canes on the bulletin boad. He's even using ornaments in our pizza jar. So I know he'll like jingle bells. And these bells will be good reminders."

"Reminders of what?" Ashley asked as she walked outside.

"Good reminders to be quiet," Alex said with a smile.

Adam rolled his eyes at me as he slipped on his backpack. I hoped Alex was right.

Alex jingled with every step we took. At first, I liked the sound. It reminded me of Santa Claus. But I didn't like them so much by the time we got to school.

Adam stopped before we went inside Mr. Parker's classroom. "Remember," he told Alex. "We have to be good."

Ashley shook her finger in front of Alex's nose. "If you're not good, we won't get ornaments in the jar."

"And then we won't get a pizza party," I added.

Alex nodded. When she did, the bells in her hair jingled. "I know," she told us. "I won't forget."

Then we all walked into the classroom.

As soon as we did, Mr. Parker stopped writing on the board. He turned and looked at Alex and her jingle bells.

A girl named Barbara giggled, but Randy put his finger on his lips. "Shhh," he warned. Then he pointed to the jar on Mr. Parker's desk. We needed a lot more ornaments before we could have a pizza party.

Adam, Ashley, and I went straight to our seats. I took out a book and pretended to read. Our whole class was quiet. Everybody, that is, except Alex.

Alex tried to be quiet. She tiptoed all the way to her desk. But she jingled with every step.

"Shhh," Randy hissed again.

Alex stuck out her tongue at him and sat down. I peeked at Mr. Parker. He was still watching Alex, but he didn't say anything. I hoped Alex was right about Mr. Parker's liking jingle bells.

3

Jingle Bells

Everybody sat still for silent reading. We all had books on our desk. Even Alex. Mr. Parker smiled. He held up a big sign. In huge purple letters it said: VERY GOOD!

Then Mr. Parker dropped a tiny ornament in the jar.

Mr. Parker wrote a sentence on the board. "There are mistakes in this sentence," he told us. "Raise your hand if you can tell me what is wrong."

Fifteen hands shot up in the air. Mr. Parker called on a girl named Maria.

"It should start with a capital letter," Maria said. Mr. Parker handed her a piece of chalk. Maria wrote a wobbly capital letter on the board.

"Very good," Mr. Parker said. Then he added, "I like the way you are all raising your hands." Mr. Parker dropped an ornament in our pizza jar.

"Who can find another mistake in this sentence?" Mr. Parker asked.

More hands went up in the air. Even Alex's. She waved her hand extra hard, but Mr. Parker called on Barbara. Barbara stood up and walked to the front of the class. She reached for the piece of chalk in Mr. Parker's hand. Barbara opened her mouth. But when she did, Alex jumped up.

"A period!" Alex blurted. "The sentence needs a period!"

Mr. Parker frowned at Alex. "Calling out answers is not the way to earn

15

ornaments," he reminded her. Then Mr. Parker took an ornament out of the jar.

Everybody looked at Alex. Alex looked down at her toes. With Alex in our class, earning a pizza party was going to be hard. Terribly hard!

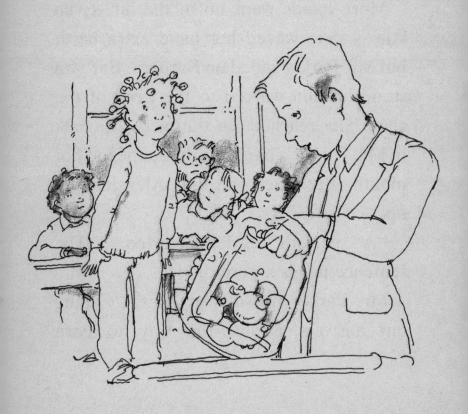

At recess, Adam and Ashley pulled Alex away from a game of soccer. I followed them.

"You have to be quiet for the rest of the day," Adam told her. "Or else we'll lose more ornaments."

"Don't say a word," I said, "unless you raise your hand."

"She can't do it," Ashley said. Ashley put her hands on her hips. "Alex doesn't know how to be quiet."

Alex stuck out her chin. "I won't say a word. You wait and see." Then she stomped away. She jingled all the way to the school doors. I like Alex. She's my best friend. But Ashley was right. Alex could never stay quiet for long.

After recess, Mr. Parker wrote ten math problems on the board. I worked hard to copy them on my paper.

I was good at math, but not as good as Adam. Adam was almost done and I was still trying to figure out the third one.

Alex wasn't very good in math. She chewed on the end of her eraser and she

scribbled on her paper. She shook her head. When she did, she jingled. Then she erased her scribbles. She jingled even more.

Randy looked at Alex. So did Barbara and Maria. "Shhh," Randy warned. But Alex was too busy to notice.

Alex tried counting on her fingers. Then

she tapped her pencil on the desk. She wiggled in her chair. She jingled with every move she made.

Mr. Parker looked up from the papers he was grading. He looked right at Alex. Then he took a deep breath and started making red marks on the papers again. He didn't put a single ornament in our pizza jar.

By the end of the day, we hadn't earned another ornament for our pizza party. Before we left Mr. Parker cleared his throat. Then he wrote with a fat black marker. He held up his new sign. It said:

NO MORE JiNGLE BELLS!

Good Behavior

I followed Alex outside to the playground. Adam and Ashley were right behind.

"It's all your fault," Ashley said. "Your jingle bells kept us from earning pizza party points!"

"But I didn't say a single word," Alex told them. "Just like I promised!"

"Alex is right," I said. "She didn't say anything."

"But her jingle bells did!" Adam said. "They made too much noise."

"Everything Alex does makes too much noise," Ashley added.

When Adam gets mad he says things that make Alex mad. Adam was mad now. "We'll never earn enough ornaments as long as Alex is in our classroom," he said.

Alex jingled when she stomped her foot. "That's not true, is it Sam?"

Alex looked at me. So did Adam and Ashley. I like Ashley and Adam. But when they gang up on Alex there is bound to be trouble.

I didn't answer Alex. Instead, I looked up in the sky. It was snowing. It had been

snowing since lunchtime. "Let's forget about jingle bells," I said. "Let's play in the snow."

"All right!" Alex said. She jumped up and her bells jingled. They sounded like sleigh bells. "Last one to their sled is a rotten egg!"

We ran all the way home. I got my sled and gave my dog Cleo a ride over to the

Tuckers' backyard. Actually, my sled is not a real sled. It's just a big piece of plastic that's curled on one end, but it really slides.

The Tuckers were already sliding down the little hill in their backyard. "Yee-haw!" Alex yelled. She twirled around and around on her sled. Her sled is the lid of a garbage can.

"Awww!" Ashley screamed as she landed in a heap at the bottom of the hill. Her shiny green plastic sled landed right on top of her. *Bump!* In two seconds, Adam smashed into her with his big piece of plastic.

Adam and Alex jumped up and raced back up the hill. "Come on," Alex called.

Cleo barked and ran up the hill after Alex.

I stopped and pulled Ashley up. We got
out of the way just in time. Alex and Cleo
came sailing down the hill together. Cleo
howled and Alex jingled. They looked like
a crazy elf and reindeer.

Down the hill we flew all afternoon. The wind whipped our faces. "This is like flying!" I told Alex. Sometimes I would pretend my sled was an airplane. I zipped through the sky with Cleo, Alex, Ashley, and Adam.

Finally, I heard my dad calling. "Sam!" he yelled. "Time for supper."

I didn't want to go. But I was hungry and my face was cold. Alex looked cold, too. Her ears were bright red. Ashley, Adam, and I had on hats. But not Alex. A hat wouldn't fit over her jingle bells.

I just hoped that tomorrow Alex would forget her jingle bells. If she didn't, we'd never earn our pizza party.

Ah-Choo!

The next morning Alex's jingle bells didn't come to school. Neither did Alex.

"Where's Alex?" I asked Ashley and Adam as we walked to school through the snow.

"She's sick," Adam explained.

I couldn't believe my ears. "Alex is never sick," I said.

Ashley pulled her hat down over her blond hair. "She's sick today. I told her she should have worn a hat yesterday. But she wouldn't listen."

"Now, she's sneezing all over the place," Adam said.

"Ah-choo here and ah-choo there," Ashley said after we went into school. "She's probably trying to get us sick, too."

It was strange to be in school without Alex. I didn't miss the jingle bells, but I did miss Alex. No one whispered to me when they weren't supposed to talk.

No one called out answers at the wrong time. So Mr. Parker put more ornaments in our jar. Everyone did their work. Mr. Parker put more ornaments in our jar. He didn't take any out. By the end of the day the jar was full.

Everyone was quiet when Mr. Parker held the jar in front of the class. Mr. Parker cleared his throat and looked around the room. "I'm very proud of you," he said. "Do you know what this means?"

I smiled at Adam. He gave me the thumbs-up sign. Ashley patted Adam on

the back. The whole class was smiling and giggling.

Mr. Parker set the jar down and wrote on the board in big letters:

PIZZA PARTY — TOMORROW!

We all cheered and clapped our hands.

"The pizza party is the best thing that's

happened all year," I told Adam and Ashley when we were walking home from school.

"It's perfect," Ashley agreed.

"There's only one thing that could ruin it," Adam said, looking up at the still-falling snow.

"What?" Ashley and I asked together.

"Snow," Adam said. "If it keeps snowing, school will be canceled along with our pizza party!"

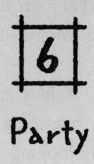

Party

"Yummy!" Alex said. A big string of cheese ran from her mouth to her pizza slice. Alex slowly chewed the cheese string. Luckily, the snow had stopped. School hadn't been canceled. Neither had the pizza party. Mr. Parker and Barbara's mother walked around the room passing out slices of pizza.

Ashley wiped her mouth with a napkin and smiled at Barbara. "Please thank your mother for the pizza. It must be nice owning a pizza store."

"You can have pizza whenever you want," I told Barbara.

Alex smacked her lips, then sneezed. "No fair, we have to earn our pizza."

Ashley looked at Alex. "You didn't earn anything. We earned the pizza."

"I helped," Alex said. "Didn't I, Sam?"

I didn't know what to say. I bit into my pizza and chewed instead.

Adam shook his head and looked at Alex. "The only reason we're having this party is because you got sick."

Alex slapped her desk with her hand. "That isn't true," she said. "Is it, Sam?"

Suddenly, my pizza didn't taste very good. I felt a little sick. I knew what Ashley and Adam said was true. But I didn't want to hurt Alex's feelings. "I'm sure we would have had the party anyway," I said slowly.

"We would have died of old age waiting for Alex to be good," Ashley said.

Mr. Parker tapped the little bell on his desk. He always rings his bell when he's upset. He was looking straight at us, and he didn't look happy.

"Alex didn't help at all," Barbara told him.

Randy nodded. "She shouldn't get any of our pizza."

Alex stood up. Her eyes got big and she snapped her fingers in front of her nose. I knew what that meant. Alex had a brilliant idea. And that meant trouble!

7

Saturday Snow

Alex wouldn't tell me her brilliant idea. She said that I had to wait and see. She had a plan.

The next day, big, fluffy snowflakes piled up on the ground. I watched Saturday morning cartoons until I heard something funny. It sounded like a sick reindeer blowing its nose.

I bundled up in my warmest clothes. I
tied a red scarf around Cleo's neck. Then
we went outside. That's when I saw what
was making the noise. It was Alex.

Alex had a big silver shovel. She was
using it to bulldoze snow off Mrs. Cooper's
driveway. With every shovelful, Alex
grunted. Then she leaned on the shovel

and breathed hard before trying to move another mound of snow.

I kicked through the snow until I was standing by Alex. "Hi, Alex," I said.

"Ah-choo!" she said. Alex wiped her nose on her coat sleeve. The tip of her nose was red, but the rest of her face looked very white.

"What are you doing?" I asked her. I had never seen Alex work on a Saturday morning. Her favorite thing in the whole world is Saturday morning cartoons.

"This is my plan," she said. Only her nose was all stopped up and it sounded more like, "Dis is by plad."

"What plan?" I asked.

Alex bulldozed another strip of snow before answering. Cleo had to jump out

of her way. "My plan to earn a pizza party all by myself," Alex finally told me.

"How will shoveling snow do that?" I asked. "I thought you had to be good to get pizza."

Alex sniffled. "Being good is just one way," she told me. "But I'm going to get my pizza by earning money. Mrs. Cooper is paying me to shovel her driveway."

I looked at Mrs. Cooper's driveway. It was piled high with snow. I looked where Alex had shoveled. It was only a small spot. I looked back at Alex. She was breathing very hard.

"This looks like hard work," I said, "and you still look sick. You should be inside."

"Ah-choo," was all Alex said. Then she dragged the shovel through the snow again.

I knew Alex was in trouble. I had to do something.

8

Pizza Plan

I trudged over to the Tuckers' house. It was hard to walk through all that snow. Adam opened the door.

"Do you know about Alex's plan?" I asked.

Adam shrugged. "It was a silly plan. Alex can't earn a pizza all by herself."

I thought for a minute. Shoveling snow

was hard work, and Alex was sick. But it was a good plan.

"I have an idea," I said to Adam. I whispered it to him. At first, Adam didn't look very happy. Then I told him we'd all get pizza, and he agreed in a hurry.

Adam got Ashley and they both bundled up. We sneaked out of the house and walked all over our neighborhood. We told all the kids in Mr. Parker's class our plan. We even went to Mr. Parker's apartment. He liked our idea so much he put on his coat and came outside to help.

We worked hard all day shoveling walks. We gave Mr. Parker the money we earned. He tucked it carefully in his wallet and smiled at us.

I followed Adam and Ashley to their house for hot chocolate. Alex was sleeping on the couch. Mrs. Tucker said Alex came home much earlier. She didn't look very good. We were very quiet so she could sleep.

On Monday morning Alex's nose still looked red, but she was feeling much

better. She sneezed only once on our way to school.

I grinned the whole way, but I didn't tell her our secret.

Mr. Parker smiled when he saw Alex. He was glad she was feeling better, too.

That afternoon Mr. Parker walked to the door to the classroom. "We have a special treat today," Mr. Parker said. "Thanks to Alex Tucker."

We all looked at Alex and grinned.

"I didn't do anything!" Alex said. "I was being good."

Mr. Parker nodded. "And your shoveling idea was good, too," he said.

Alex frowned. "But I was too sick to finish. I never earned my pizza party."

"Yes, you did!" Mr. Parker said. He smiled and opened the classroom door.

Barbara's mother stood in the doorway. She held six big pizza boxes.

Everybody yelled, "Surprise!"

"We finished the shoveling," I told Alex. "We helped you earn the party!"

"Congratulations!" Mr. Parker said. "I'm proud of the way you worked together to be such good friends. Everybody in the class earned this party!"

Alex and Ashley slapped each other on the back. Barbara's mom handed me the biggest slice of pizza. I looked at Alex. She smiled so big I could see the space where her tooth used to be. I smiled back. Being friends with the Tucker Triplets is terrific. Even greater than pizza!